Bless Yourself with Money

5 Powerful Tools for Creating Lasting Wealth

An Amazing Journey to Wealth Creation

Michael J. Seid

Contents

Michael writes on various topics including physical and mental well-being. He has a holistic approach to life and this book is another proof of that. Financial independence and prosperity is part of overall well-being, which contributes to happiness.

Discover the secrets to creating lasting wealth and prosperity by harnessing the power of five transformative tools: gratitude, charity, investment, learning, and visualization. This comprehensive guide provides a holistic approach to wealth creation, going beyond traditional financial advice to help you cultivate a mindset of abundance and prosperity.

Part 1: Gratitude - The Foundation of Wealth

Explore the profound impact of gratitude on your financial life, and learn practical strategies for cultivating a gratitude practice that attracts abundance and prosperity.

Part 2: Charity - The Power of Giving

Discover how charitable giving can not only benefit others, but also create a positive feedback loop of abundance and prosperity in your own life.

Part 3: Investment - Growing Your Wealth

Get expert advice on investing in stocks, real

estate, and other assets, as well as strategies for managing risk and maximizing returns. Explore alternative investment options, such as social impact investing and crowdfunding.

Part 4: Learning - The Key to Unlocking New Opportunities

Learn how to stay ahead of the curve by continuously updating your skills and knowledge..

Part 5: Visualization - The Power of Mind Over Money

Discover the science behind visualization and how it can be used to reprogram your mind for wealth and success. Learn practical exercises and techniques for visualizing your financial goals and overcoming self-limiting beliefs.

Conclusion:

By integrating these five tools into your life, you'll be equipped with a powerful blueprint that will help you create lasting wealth and achieve your financial goals. Whether you're just starting out or looking to take your wealth to the next level, this book offers a comprehensive and inspiring guide to achieving financial freedom and living a life of purpose and fulfilment.

Part 1: Gratitude - The Foundation of Wealth

Gratitude and wealth may seem like unrelated concepts, but research has shown that cultivating gratitude can have a positive impact on one's financial well-being. Here are some ways in which gratitude can increase wealth:

1. Shifts focus from lack to abundance: When we focus on what we're grateful for, we begin to see the abundance in our lives rather than dwelling on what's lacking. This mindset shift can help us appreciate the resources we already have, leading to a greater sense of financial security and confidence.

2. Encourages mindful spending: Practicing gratitude helps us become more mindful of our spending habits. When we're grateful for what we have, we're less likely to engage in impulsive or excessive spending, which can lead to financial waste and debt.

3. Fosters contentment: Gratitude promotes contentment with what we have, reducing the

desire for more material possessions. This contentment can lead to reduced spending and a greater sense of financial satisfaction.

4. Attracts positive relationships: Grateful people tend to attract positive relationships, which can lead to new opportunities, collaborations, and even business partnerships. These relationships can, in turn, contribute to increased wealth and financial stability.

5. Boosts creativity and resourcefulness: Gratitude can stimulate creativity and resourcefulness, helping us find innovative solutions to financial challenges. When we're grateful, we're more likely to think outside the box and explore new opportunities for generating income or reducing expenses.

6. Reduces stress and anxiety: Financial stress and anxiety can be significant obstacles to wealth creation. Gratitude practices, such as meditation or journaling, can help reduce stress and anxiety, allowing us to approach financial decisions with a clearer mind and greater confidence.

7. Increases generosity: Grateful people are more

likely to be generous, which can lead to increased wealth in the long run. When we give to others, we create a positive feedback loop of abundance, attracting more resources and opportunities into our lives.

8. Improves financial decision-making: Gratitude can help us make more informed, thoughtful financial decisions. By focusing on what we're grateful for, we're more likely to prioritize our spending and investing, making choices that align with our values and goals.

9. Enhances resilience: Gratitude can help us develop resilience in the face of financial setbacks or challenges. When we're grateful, we're better equipped to bounce back from adversity, adapt to changing circumstances, and find opportunities for growth and learning.

10. Aligns with abundance mindset: Gratitude is a key component of an abundance mindset, which is essential for attracting wealth and financial success. When we focus on gratitude, we begin to see the world as a place of abundance, rather than scarcity, and we're more likely to take risks,

invest in ourselves, and pursue opportunities that can lead to increased wealth.

Practicing gratitude is a powerful way to cultivate a positive mindset and attract wealth into your life. Here are some ways to practice gratitude for wealth creation:

1. Gratitude Journal: Keep a gratitude journal to write down things you're thankful for each day. This can include material possessions, relationships, health, or anything else that brings you joy.

2. Morning Gratitude: Start your day by expressing gratitude for the things you already have in your life. This can be done through a morning meditation, prayer, or simply taking a few minutes to reflect on the things you're thankful for.

3. Gratitude Jar: Create a gratitude jar where you write down things you're thankful for on slips of paper and put them in the jar. Read them when you need a reminder of the good things in your life.

4. Share Gratitude: Express gratitude to others by writing thank-you notes, giving compliments, or simply telling someone how much you appreciate them.

5. Focus on Abundance: Focus on the abundance you already have in your life, rather than what's lacking. This can help shift your mindset from scarcity to abundance.

6. Gratitude Meditation: Practice a gratitude meditation by focusing on the things you're thankful for and visualizing them in your mind.

7. Gratitude Affirmations: Repeat gratitude affirmations, such as "I am grateful for all the abundance in my life," to help reprogram your mind with a positive and grateful attitude.

8. Reflect on Past Blessings: Reflect on past blessings and experiences that have brought you joy and gratitude. This can help you appreciate the present moment and attract more positivity into your life.

9. Practice Mindfulness: Practice mindfulness by being present in the moment and appreciating the small things in life. This can help you cultivate a sense of gratitude and appreciation for the world around you.

Remember, gratitude is a muscle that needs to be exercised regularly. By incorporating these practices into your daily routine, you can cultivate a positive and grateful mindset that can help attract wealth and abundance into your life.

Tips for Practicing Gratitude for Wealth Creation:

1. Be specific: Be specific about what you're grateful for, such as a specific amount of money or a particular material possession.

2. Focus on the present: Focus on the present moment and what you're grateful for, rather than dwelling on the past or worrying about the future.

3. Use positive language: Use positive language when expressing gratitude, such as "I am grateful for" instead of "I don't have enough."

4. Make it a habit: Make gratitude a habit by incorporating it into your daily routine, such as right before bed or first thing in the morning.

5. Share with others: Share your gratitude with others, such as by writing a thank-you note or giving a compliment, to help spread positivity and attract more abundance into your life.

By practicing gratitude and cultivating a positive mindset, you can attract more wealth and abundance into your life and achieve your financial goals.

In summary, gratitude can increase wealth by shifting our focus from lack to abundance, encouraging mindful spending, fostering contentment, and attracting positive relationships. By cultivating gratitude, we can develop a more positive and resilient mindset, leading to better financial decision-making, increased creativity, and a greater sense of financial well-being.

Part 2: Charity - The Power of Giving

Charity and wealth may seem like unrelated concepts, but research has shown that giving to others can have a positive impact on one's financial well-being. Here are some ways in which charity can increase wealth:

1. Tax benefits: Charitable donations can provide tax deductions, which can reduce taxable income and lower tax liability. This can result in more money in your pocket, which can be invested or saved.

2. Networking opportunities: Engaging in charitable activities can provide opportunities to meet new people, including potential business partners, investors, or clients. These connections can lead to new business opportunities, collaborations, or investments that can increase wealth.

3. Personal growth and development: Charity work can help individuals develop new skills, such as leadership, communication, and problem-

solving. These skills can be valuable in personal and professional life, leading to increased earning potential and wealth.

4. Social capital: Charity work can help build social capital, which refers to the networks, relationships, and reputation that can provide access to resources, opportunities, and support. Social capital can be a valuable asset in achieving financial success.

5. Increased gratitude and positivity: Giving to others can increase feelings of gratitude and positivity, which can lead to a more optimistic outlook on life and a greater sense of financial well-being. This, in turn, can lead to better financial decision-making and a greater willingness to take calculated risks.

6. Spiritual benefits: Many people believe that giving to others can have spiritual benefits, such as attracting positive energy, good fortune, or abundance into their lives. While this may not be measurable, it can have a profound impact on one's mindset and behaviour, leading to increased wealth and financial success.

7. Legacy and impact: Charity work can provide a sense of purpose and fulfilment, which can lead to a greater sense of legacy and impact. This can motivate individuals to work harder, invest wisely, and build wealth that can be passed on to future generations.

8. Access to new markets and opportunities: Charity work can provide access to new markets, industries, or opportunities that may not have been available otherwise. This can lead to new business ventures, investments, or partnerships that can increase wealth.

9. Improved mental and physical health: Giving to others has been shown to have positive effects on mental and physical health, including reduced stress, anxiety, and depression. This can lead to increased productivity, better financial decision-making, and a greater sense of financial well-being.

10. Abundance mindset: Charity work can help cultivate an abundance mindset, which is essential for attracting wealth and financial success. When

we focus on giving to others, we begin to see the world as a place of abundance, rather than scarcity, and we're more likely to take risks, invest in ourselves, and pursue opportunities that can lead to increased wealth.

In summary, charity can increase wealth by providing tax benefits, networking opportunities, personal growth and development, social capital, increased gratitude and positivity, spiritual benefits, legacy and impact, access to new markets and opportunities, improved mental and physical health, and an abundance mindset. By giving to others, we can create a positive feedback loop of abundance, attracting more resources, opportunities, and wealth into our lives.

There are various investment strategies that can produce wealth, each with its own unique characteristics, risks, and potential returns. Here are some common investment strategies and how they can produce wealth:

1. Diversified Stock Portfolio: Investing in a diversified portfolio of stocks can provide long-term growth and wealth creation. By spreading investments across different asset classes, sectors, and geographies, investors can reduce risk and increase potential returns.

2. Real Estate Investing: Investing in real estate can provide a steady stream of income and long-term appreciation in property value. Strategies like rental properties, real estate investment trusts (REITs), and real estate crowdfunding can help investors build wealth.

3. Dividend Investing: Investing in dividend-paying stocks can provide a regular income stream and potentially lower volatility. By reinvesting dividends, investors can benefit from

compounding returns and long-term wealth creation.

4. Growth Investing: Investing in growth stocks, such as those in emerging industries or with high growth potential, can provide significant returns over the long term. However, this strategy comes with higher risks and requires a longer investment horizon.

5. Index Fund Investing: Investing in index funds, which track a specific market index like the S&P 500, can provide broad diversification and potentially lower fees. This strategy can help investors build wealth over the long term while minimizing risk.

6. Value Investing: Investing in undervalued stocks, such as those with low price-to-earnings ratios, can provide opportunities for long-term growth and wealth creation. Value investors seek to buy stocks at a discount and sell them at a higher price, earning a profit.

7. Peer-to-Peer Lending: Investing in peer-to-peer

lending platforms, which connect borrowers with investors, can provide regular income and potentially higher returns than traditional fixed-income investments.

8. Cryptocurrency Investing: Investing in cryptocurrencies, such as Bitcoin or Ethereum, can provide potentially high returns, but also comes with significant risks and volatility.

9. Private Equity Investing: Investing in private equity funds or directly in private companies can provide opportunities for long-term growth and wealth creation. However, this strategy requires significant capital and comes with higher risks.

10. Hedge Fund Investing: Investing in hedge funds, which use alternative investment strategies to generate returns, can provide potentially higher returns and lower volatility. However, this strategy requires significant capital and comes with higher fees.

11. Robo-Advisory Investing: Investing in robo-advisory platforms, which use algorithms to

manage investment portfolios, can provide low-cost, diversified investment options and potentially higher returns over the long term.

12. Tax-Advantaged Investing: Investing in tax-advantaged accounts, such as 401(k) or IRA, can provide tax benefits and potentially higher returns over the long term.

13. Impact Investing: Investing in companies or projects that generate social or environmental impact, alongside financial returns, can provide a sense of purpose and potentially higher returns over the long term.

14. Commodity Investing: Investing in commodities, such as gold or oil, can provide a hedge against inflation and potentially higher returns over the long term.

15. Forex Investing: Investing in foreign currencies, such as through forex trading, can provide potentially high returns, but also comes with significant risks and volatility.

Crowdfunding is a way to raise money from a large number of people, typically through an online platform. It allows individuals, businesses, and organizations to fund their projects, products, or causes by collecting small contributions from a large number of people, often in exchange for rewards or equity.

There are several types of crowdfunding, including:

1. Donation-based crowdfunding: This type of crowdfunding involves raising money for a cause or project without offering any rewards or equity in return. Platforms like GoFundMe and Kickstarter are popular for donation-based crowdfunding.

2. Rewards-based crowdfunding: This type of crowdfunding involves offering rewards to backers in exchange for their contributions. Rewards can range from early access to a product or service to exclusive merchandise or experiences. Platforms like Kickstarter and Indiegogo are popular for rewards-based crowdfunding.

3. Equity-based crowdfunding: This type of crowdfunding involves offering equity in a company or project to backers in exchange for their contributions. Platforms like Seedrs and Crowdfunder are popular for equity-based crowdfunding.

4. Lending-based crowdfunding: This type of crowdfunding involves lending money to individuals or businesses, with the expectation of being repaid with interest. Platforms like Lending Club and Prosper are popular for lending-based crowdfunding.

Crowdfunding has become a popular way to raise money for a wide range of projects and causes, including:

1. Creative projects: Crowdfunding has been used to fund films, music, art, and other creative projects.

2. Business startups: Crowdfunding has been used to fund business startups, including tech companies, restaurants, and retail stores.

3. Social causes: Crowdfunding has been used to raise money for social causes, including charities, non-profits, and community projects.

4. Personal projects: Crowdfunding has been used to fund personal projects, including medical expenses, education, and travel.

The benefits of crowdfunding include:

1. Access to funding: Crowdfunding provides access to funding for projects and causes that may not have been eligible for traditional funding.

2. Community engagement: Crowdfunding allows creators to engage with their community and build a loyal following.

3. Marketing and promotion: Crowdfunding platforms provide a built-in marketing and promotion tool, helping creators to reach a wider audience.

4. Flexibility: Crowdfunding allows creators to set

their own funding goals and deadlines, providing flexibility and control over the funding process.

However, crowdfunding also has its challenges and risks, including:

1. Competition: Crowdfunding platforms are highly competitive, with many projects and causes vying for attention and funding.

2. Fees: Crowdfunding platforms often charge fees, which can eat into the funding raised.

3. Risk of failure: Crowdfunding projects can fail to reach their funding goals, or may not deliver on their promises.

4. Regulatory risks: Crowdfunding is subject to regulatory risks, including changes in laws and regulations that can impact the funding process.

Overall, crowdfunding has become a popular and effective way to raise money for a wide range of projects and causes. However, it's essential to carefully consider the benefits and risks, and to choose a reputable and suitable crowdfunding platform for your needs.

Each investment strategy has its unique characteristics, risks, and potential returns. It's essential to understand the strategy, assess personal risk tolerance, and diversify investments to achieve long-term wealth creation. Additionally, investors should consider factors like fees, taxes, and inflation when selecting an investment strategy.

Part 4: Learning - The Key to Unlocking New Opportunities

Learning can increase wealth in numerous ways, including:

1. Improved career prospects: Acquiring new skills and knowledge can lead to better job opportunities, higher salaries, and greater career advancement, ultimately resulting in increased wealth.

2. Increased earning potential: Learning can enhance earning potential by providing individuals with the skills and expertise needed to take on higher-paying jobs or start their own businesses.

3. Entrepreneurial opportunities: Learning about entrepreneurship, business management, and industry trends can equip individuals with the knowledge and skills necessary to start and grow a successful business, generating wealth through profits.

4. Investment knowledge: Learning about

investing, personal finance, and money management can help individuals make informed investment decisions, potentially leading to increased wealth through smart investing.

5. Networking opportunities: Learning can provide opportunities to connect with like-minded individuals, industry experts, and potential mentors, which can lead to valuable relationships, partnerships, and business opportunities.

6. Personal development: Learning can lead to personal growth, increased confidence, and improved self-discipline, all of which are essential for achieving financial success and building wealth.

7. Access to new markets and industries: Learning about emerging trends, technologies, and industries can provide individuals with the knowledge and skills needed to tap into new markets and capitalize on new opportunities, potentially generating wealth.

8. Improved financial literacy: Learning about

personal finance, budgeting, and money management can help individuals make informed financial decisions, avoid debt, and build wealth over time.

9. Increased productivity: Learning can help individuals become more efficient and productive, allowing them to accomplish more in less time and potentially earn more money.

10. Staying ahead of the curve: Continuous learning can help individuals stay up-to-date with the latest trends, technologies, and industry developments, enabling them to adapt and thrive in a rapidly changing world and potentially increasing their wealth.

11. Developing multiple income streams: Learning can provide individuals with the skills and knowledge needed to create multiple income streams, such as starting a side business, investing in real estate, or generating passive income through online courses or affiliate marketing.

12. Building a valuable skillset: Learning can help

individuals develop a valuable skillset that is in high demand, making them more attractive to employers and potentially leading to higher salaries and increased wealth.

13. Creating intellectual property: Learning can enable individuals to create intellectual property, such as books, courses, or software, which can generate passive income and increase wealth.

14. Improving negotiation skills: Learning can help individuals develop effective negotiation skills, enabling them to secure better deals, higher salaries, and more favorable contracts, ultimately increasing their wealth.

15. Reducing financial stress: Learning about personal finance and money management can help individuals reduce financial stress, make informed financial decisions, and build wealth over time.

In summary, learning can increase wealth by providing individuals with the skills, knowledge, and expertise needed to succeed in their careers, start and grow businesses, make informed investment decisions, and build multiple income streams.

Visualization is a powerful technique that can help create wealth by reprogramming the mind to focus on abundance, prosperity, and financial success. Here are some ways visualization can create wealth:

1. Clarifies financial goals: Visualization helps individuals clarify their financial goals, making it easier to focus on what they want to achieve. By vividly imagining their desired financial outcomes, they can create a clear mental picture of their goals.

2. Reprograms the subconscious mind: Visualization can reprogram the subconscious mind to believe in abundance and prosperity, rather than scarcity and limitation. This helps to overcome negative thought patterns and self-doubt that may be holding them back from achieving financial success.

3. Increases motivation and drive: Visualization can increase motivation and drive by creating a sense of excitement and anticipation for achieving financial goals. By vividly imagining themselves achieving success, individuals can tap into their inner motivation and drive.

4. Enhances creativity and innovation: Visualization can enhance creativity and innovation by allowing individuals to imagine new and innovative solutions to financial challenges. By thinking outside the box and exploring new possibilities, they can create new opportunities for wealth creation.

5. Attracts abundance and prosperity: Visualization can attract abundance and prosperity by emitting a positive energy frequency that resonates with the universe. By focusing on abundance and prosperity, individuals can attract more of it into their lives.

6. Builds confidence and self-esteem: Visualization can build confidence and self-esteem by helping individuals imagine themselves achieving financial

success. By vividly imagining their accomplishments, they can develop a stronger sense of self-worth and confidence.

7. Overcomes fear and anxiety: Visualization can overcome fear and anxiety by helping individuals imagine themselves successfully navigating financial challenges. By vividly imagining positive outcomes, they can build resilience and develop a more positive mindset.

8. Creates a positive mindset: Visualization can create a positive mindset by focusing on abundance, prosperity, and financial success. By cultivating a positive mindset, individuals can attract more positive experiences and opportunities into their lives.

9. Enhances intuition and instinct: Visualization can enhance intuition and instinct by allowing individuals to tap into their inner wisdom and guidance. By trusting their intuition and instinct, they can make more informed financial decisions and avoid costly mistakes.

10. Accelerates manifestation: Visualization can accelerate manifestation by focusing energy and attention on specific financial goals. By vividly imagining their desired outcomes, individuals can bring their goals into reality more quickly and efficiently.

11. Increases gratitude and appreciation: Visualization can increase gratitude and appreciation by helping individuals focus on the abundance and prosperity they already have in their lives. By cultivating gratitude and appreciation, they can attract more abundance and prosperity into their lives.

12. Supports smart financial decisions: Visualization can support smart financial decisions by helping individuals imagine the potential consequences of their financial choices. By vividly imagining different scenarios, they can make more informed decisions and avoid costly mistakes.

13. Fosters a growth mindset: Visualization can foster a growth mindset by helping individuals

imagine themselves learning, growing, and evolving. By embracing a growth mindset, they can stay adaptable and open to new opportunities and experiences.

14. Enhances resilience and adaptability: Visualization can enhance resilience and adaptability by helping individuals imagine themselves navigating financial challenges and setbacks. By developing resilience and adaptability, they can bounce back from adversity and stay focused on their financial goals.

15. Creates a sense of purpose and meaning: Visualization can create a sense of purpose and meaning by helping individuals imagine themselves achieving their financial goals and living a fulfilling life. By cultivating a sense of purpose and meaning, they can stay motivated and focused on their financial objectives.

Here are some visualization techniques that can help with wealth creation:

1. Morning Visualization: Start your day by visualizing yourself already in possession of the

wealth and success you desire. See yourself waking up in a beautiful home, with a sense of abundance and prosperity surrounding you.

2. Mind Movie: Create a mental movie of yourself achieving your financial goals. Imagine yourself working towards your goals, overcoming obstacles, and celebrating your successes.

3. Vision Board: Create a physical or digital vision board that represents your financial goals. Include images, words, and phrases that evoke feelings of abundance and prosperity.

4. Gratitude Visualization: Visualize yourself feeling grateful for the wealth and abundance you already have in your life. See yourself surrounded by the things you're thankful for, and feel a sense of appreciation and abundance.

5. Abundance Meditation: Meditate on the feeling of abundance and prosperity. Imagine yourself surrounded by a warm, golden light that represents abundance and wealth.

6. Future Self: Visualize yourself in the future, having already achieved your financial goals. See yourself living a life of abundance and prosperity, and feel a sense of pride and accomplishment.

7. Wealth Scenario: Visualize a specific scenario where you're enjoying the fruits of your labour. Imagine yourself on a luxurious vacation, or living in a beautiful home, or driving a fancy car.

8. Prosperity Walk: Take a walk while visualizing yourself in a state of prosperity and abundance. Imagine yourself walking through a beautiful, lush environment, surrounded by abundance and wealth.

9. Visualization Journaling: Write down your visualization experiences in a journal. Reflect on what you saw, felt, and experienced during your visualization, and use it as a tool to track your progress.

10. Guided Visualization: Listen to guided visualization recordings that are specifically

designed to help you visualize wealth and abundance. These recordings can help you relax and focus your mind on your financial goals.

Remember, the key to successful visualization is to be consistent, persistent, and patient. Make visualization a regular part of your daily routine, and watch your mindset and circumstances transform over time.

Additionally, here are some tips to enhance your visualization practice:

- Be specific: Clearly define what you want to achieve through your visualization practice.
- Use all your senses: Incorporate all your senses into your visualization, including sight, sound, touch, taste, and smell.
- Emotional connection: Connect with the emotions of already having what you want to achieve. Feel the excitement, joy, and gratitude of having achieved your goals.
- Consistency: Make visualization a regular part of your daily routine, ideally at the same time every day.
- Patience: Visualization is a practice that takes time to develop. Be patient and consistent, and

you'll start to see results over time.

By incorporating these visualization techniques into your daily routine, you can start to shift your mindset and attract wealth and abundance into your life.

In summary, visualization can create wealth by reprogramming the mind to focus on abundance, prosperity, and financial success. By vividly imagining their desired financial outcomes, individuals can clarify their goals, build confidence and motivation, and attract more abundance and prosperity into their lives.